LEVEL 2 SCIENCE

LET'S READ AND FIND OUT

HOW MOUNTAINS ARE MADE

BY KATHLEEN WEIDNER ZOEHFELD

ILLUSTRATED BY JAMES GRAHAM HALE

HARPER

An Imprint of HarperCollinsPublishers

Special thanks to Dr. Harold Tobin, Chair of the Department of Geoscience at the University of Wisconsin–Madison, and Laurence Lipsett for their expert advice.

The Let's-Read-and-Find-Out Science book series was originated by Dr. Franklyn M. Branley, Astronomer Emeritus and former Chairman of the American Museum of Natural History–Hayden Planetarium, and was formerly co-edited by him and Dr. Roma Gans, Professor Emeritus of Childhood Education, Teachers College, Columbia University. Text and illustrations for each of the books in the series are checked for accuracy by an expert in the relevant field. For more information about Let's-Read-and-Find-Out Science books, write to HarperCollins Children's Books, 195 Broadway, New York, NY 10007, or visit our website at www.letsreadandfindout.com.

Let's Read-and-Find-Out Science® is a trademark of HarperCollins Publishers.

HOW MOUNTAINS ARE MADE
Text copyright © 1995 by Kathleen Weidner Zoehfeld
Illustrations copyright © 1995 by James Graham Hale
All rights reserved. Manufactured in China.
No part of this book may be used or reproduced in any manner whatsoever without written permission except in the case of brief quotations embodied in critical articles and reviews. For information address HarperCollins Children's Books, a division of HarperCollins Publishers, 195 Broadway, New York, NY 10007.
www.harpercollinschildrens.com

Library of Congress Cataloging-in-Publication Data
Zoehfeld, Kathleen Weidner.
    How mountains are made / by Kathleen Weidner Zoehfeld ; illustrated by James Graham Hale.
        p.   cm. — (Let's-read-and-find-out science. Stage 2)
    ISBN 978-0-06-238203-0
    I. Orogeny—Juvenile literature. [1. Mountains. 2. Geology.] I. Hale, James Graham, ill. II. Title. III. Series.
QE621.Z64 1995   93-45436
551.8'2—dc20   CIP
                                                                                                                   AC

22   SCP   11
❖
Revised edition, 2015

HOW MOUNTAINS ARE MADE

4

On Saturdays sometimes we go mountain climbing. We follow a trail through a thick forest.

At first the climb is easy.

Then it gets steeper and steeper. We stop on a rock ledge halfway up and eat our lunch.

When we start out again, we have to walk more slowly. The slope is getting very steep. The forest is thinning out, and the trees are shorter. We can see the top of the mountain, but it seems to take forever to get there.

When we reach the top, we can see out in every direction!
There are hardly any trees up here, and the land is rocky.

We spend a long time looking at the rocks. Here's one with the shape of a seashell in it.

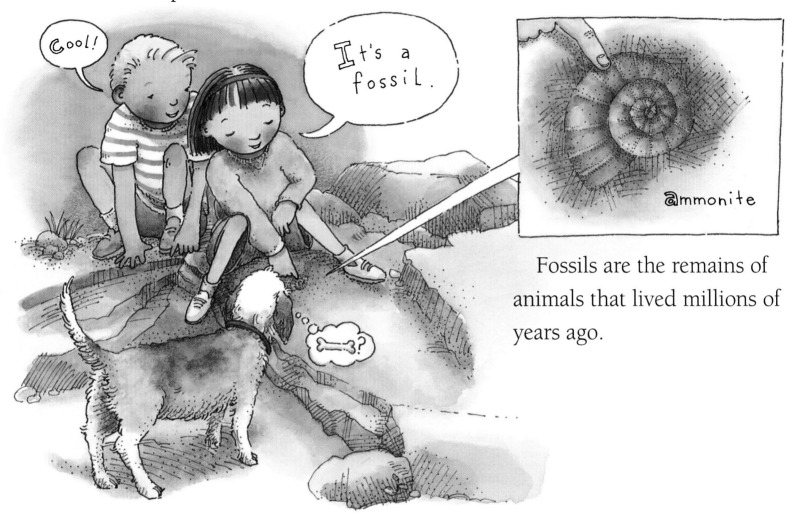

Cool!

It's a fossil.

ammonite

Fossils are the remains of animals that lived millions of years ago.

This mountain is more than four thousand feet high. That's nearly a mile. There are no oceans up here. How did a sea animal get to the top of this mountain?

The highest mountain in the world is Mount Everest, in Nepal. It is 29,028 feet high. That's almost five and a half miles. But fossil seashells have been found on Mount Everest, too.

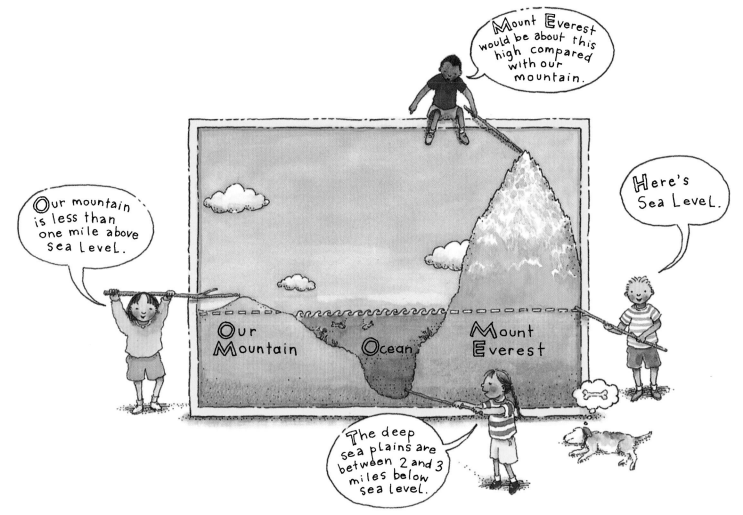

Millions of years ago Mount Everest was not a mountain at all. It was part of a flat plain under an ocean.

Our mountain was part of a flat plain under an ocean, too. All sorts of sea animals lived right here. But that was a long, long time ago. Many changes have happened since then.

The earth is always changing. Old mountains disappear.
They are worn away by ice, rain, and flowing water.

New mountains form where there were no mountains before.

We can't see the changes happening, though. Mountains
are built up and worn down gradually, over hundreds of
millions of years.

When we look at the earth, all we see are rocks and soil, and the trees and other plants growing in the soil. But if we could look inside the earth, we would see that it is made up of different layers.

The surface of the earth is the first layer. It is made of the soil and the rocks we see around us all the time.

Just under the surface is a rocky layer, about thirty-five miles thick, called the earth's crust.

Beneath the crust is a layer of rock called the mantle. The crust and the upper layer of the mantle together form a hard outer shell called the lithosphere.

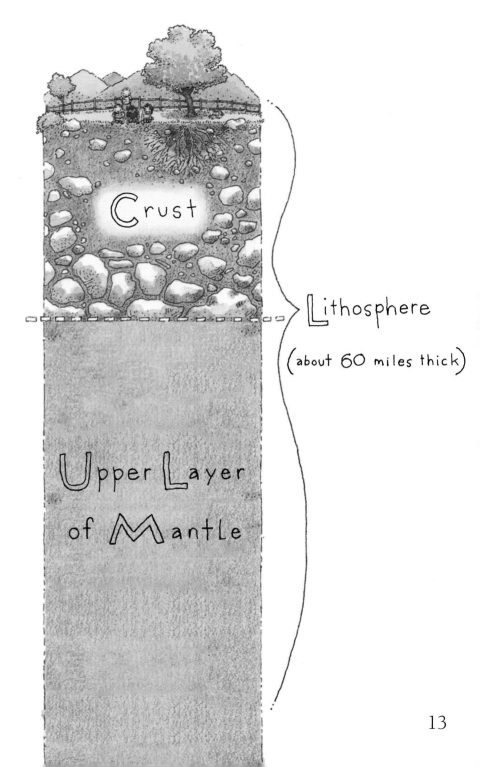

Crust

Lithosphere

(about 60 miles thick)

Upper Layer of Mantle

The lithosphere is broken into pieces called plates. The plates are huge. There are eight major plates, and several smaller ones.

Under the outer shell is a layer of hot, partly melted rock that is softer and can flow slowly, like honey. The rock plates float on top of this mushy layer. The mushy layer contains some molten rock called magma.

The plates move slowly over the mushy layer— just a few inches a year.

PLATE

PLATE

CRUST

LITHOSPHERE

MANTLE

Magma forms here.

The earth's plates are always in motion. They have been moving for hundreds of millions of years.

Most scientists believe that all the mountains on earth were formed by slow movements in the earth's outer shell.

But mountains in different parts of the world look very different from one another.

That's because in different parts of the earth the outer shell moves in different ways.

In some places two plates press against each other.

The tremendous pressure forces the crust to lift and fold over itself.

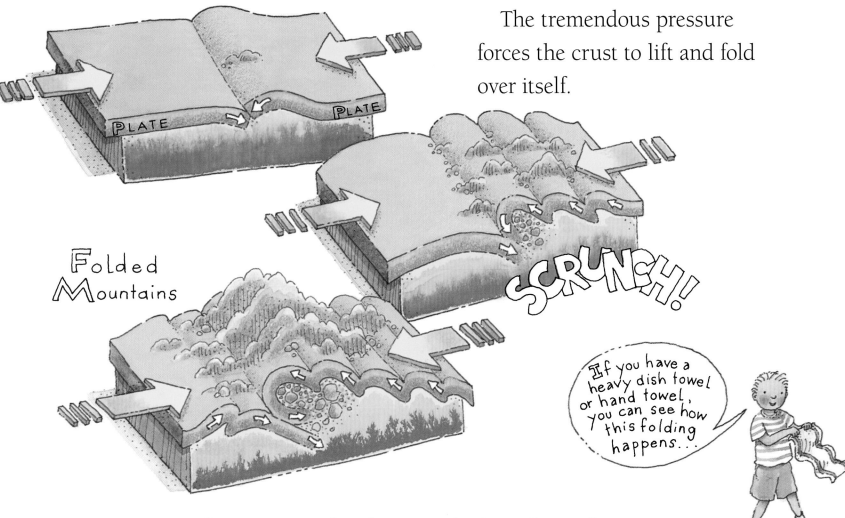

PLATE

PLATE

Folded Mountains

SCRUNCH!

If you have a heavy dish towel or hand towel, you can see how this folding happens...

Great waves of rock are pushed up. Ice and water cut through the folds to form sharp, craggy mountains.

17

Lay a towel out flat on a table. Put the palms of your hands down, one on each end of the towel.

Then, slowly slide your hands toward each other.

The folds and ridges that appear in the middle of the towel are like the folds and ridges that form giant mountains when two plates press against each other.

In other places, pressure deep within the earth pulls and stretches the crust. The stretching sometimes causes long cracks, or fault lines, to cut through the crust.

Fault-Block Mountains

The crust on one side of a crack may slide slowly upward, while the crust on the other side pushes downward. Block-shaped mountains are formed this way.

Sometimes the crust does not fold or crack. Sometimes magma pushes through a vent in the solid rock layer. It collects in a pocket under the crust.

The pocket of magma grows larger, until it bends the crust upward.

When this happens, a high dome is formed. Rain and ice wash away the softer rocks above, and rounded peaks and valleys appear.

In a few places on earth, plates are moving away from one another. This usually happens deep under the oceans.

When it hits the cool ocean water, the magma becomes solid. Great underwater mountain ranges are built up.

Once in a while a small crack, or vent, forms in the lithosphere—sometimes right in the middle of a plate. Red-hot magma pushes up through the crack.

When it gets to the surface of the earth, the magma cools and hardens.

Once Magma reaches the surface, it's called Lava.

Lava

Plate (Lithosphere)

crack

Magma

Lava and ash build up around the crack, making the land higher and higher. A cone-shaped volcanic mountain is formed.

Most volcanic mountains are formed in places where one plate pushes under another. As the edge of one plate sinks, it heats up.

The solid rock of the plate's edge melts in the intense heat. The melted rock, or magma, rushes up through weak places in the crust above.

In fiery blasts, lava is thrown onto the earth's surface. It cools and hardens, and mountains are built.

Some mountains have been around for hundreds of millions of years. Others are still being built up right now.

The mountain we climbed is an old mountain.

The fossil we found can tell us a lot about how old our mountain is.

Scientists have a special way of telling the age of a fossil. This one is nearly 280 million years old.

It died, sank to the bottom, and was buried in sand and mud. It must have been buried sometime just before our mountain began to be born.

25

So, we know that the land here began to rise around 280 million years ago. From the shape of this mountain, we can tell it was formed by a folding of the crust.

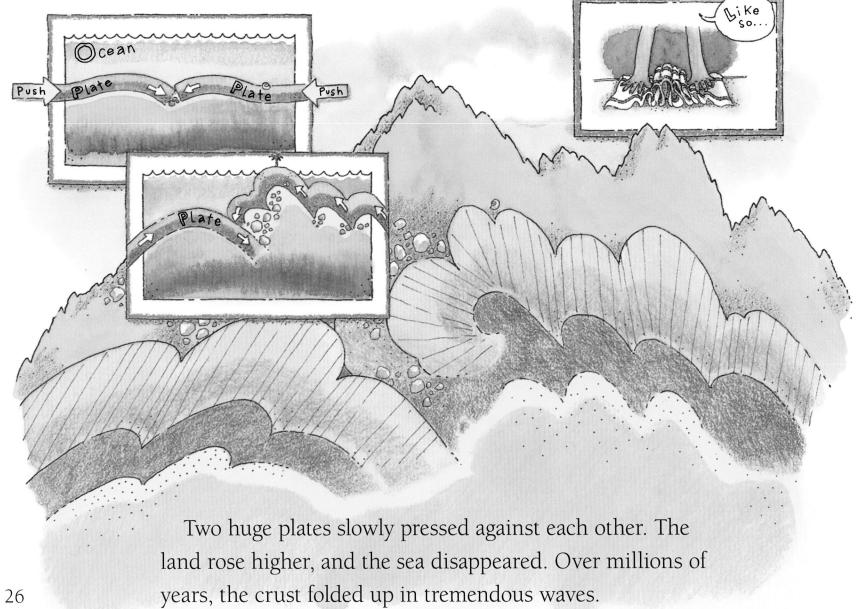

Two huge plates slowly pressed against each other. The land rose higher, and the sea disappeared. Over millions of years, the crust folded up in tremendous waves.

This mountain and the other mountains around our town were once much higher than they are now. They were sharp and craggy. Now they are lower and smoother.

For millions of years, rain, ice, and flowing water have worn our mountains down.

Millions of years from now, the rain, ice, and flowing water will have worn them down completely.

Mount Everest is a younger mountain. It is still sharp and
craggy. And it is still being pushed up higher. Mount Everest
may be growing as much as two inches each year.